A LONG HARD FALL

A Walter Anchor Ghost Detective Story, Case #3

ROBERT J. MCCARTER

Little Hummingbird Publishing

- **Case 1: Detecting Haley** (also part of *Life After: Stories of Life, Death, and the Places in Between*)
- **Case 2: The Ghost Bride's Gift**
- **Case 3: A Long Hard Fall**
- **Case 4: Death of a Dentist** (coming May, 2020)
- **Case 5: A Hollywood Kind of a Murder** (coming July 2020)
- **Case 6: The Red Arrow Murders** (coming September, 2020)
- **Unfinished Business: The Cases of Walter Anchor Ghost Detective** (coming October, 2020)

Chapter One

EMILY WAS IN A GOOD MOOD AND I DIDN'T WANT TO disappoint her, but I really wasn't up for solving another murder, especially one without a fresh ghost to tell me what had happened.

"Fascinating, right, Walter?" Emily asked, her four-year-old face sporting a big smile, her head nodding and shaking her tight blond curls. But that twinkle in her ancient green eyes spoke of a lust that no four-year-old ever experienced. Emily was four when she died, but she's been a ghost for eighty years and has seen a lot of life... well, afterlife.

I nodded and paced around the body. His manner of death was interesting—his left leg was twisted in a sickening way, the left half of his face caved in, and his torso was too damn flat. It looked like he had fallen from a great height and died on impact. But instead of being on the street, this body, dressed in a boring business suit, was on the flat white roof of one of Tucson's high-rises. There was blood here too, making it seem like this is where the death had happened, but how?

I stared up into the washed-out blue of the Tucson sky and wondered how big a drop it took to make a body look like this. It was midday, the sun right above and the air hot —not that any of us could feel it, ghosts or dead guy. And if you wanted to kill somebody this way, it would be much easier to just throw them off of a building, not drop them onto the roof of a forty-story high-rise.

"Yeah, fascinating," I said, pointing at the body, "but I don't know where we come in. Are you sure this is a fresh one?"

Emily nodded and pointed to the head where some blood was still oozing out.

"And why no ghost? A death like this, you'd think there'd be a ghost." I know if I had been dropped to my death, I'd have unresolved issues. Hell, I died from a propofol overdose—I didn't do it, it was made to look like a suicide—in my own dental office. Not a bad way to go, but enough to leave me a ghost and shove me into this whole ghost detective thing trying to solve my own murder. But we are out of clues on that, and Emily just loves doing this, and maybe the practice will help if we ever do get any leads on my death.

Emily pursed her lips and shrugged. "But fascinating, right?" The young-looking, ancient ghost has a nose for death and found us a lot of fascinating cases. But today, she was trying too hard. A recent case had veered into very personal territory and resulted in me confronting my past in the form of my ex-wife Sun. I got some closure, but it left me depressed. Emily has kept us busy with nonstop cases since then. Depression is not a good thing for a ghost. You know those cliched, gape-jawed, moaning ghosts? Get too depressed as a ghost and you just might end up like that.

"Hon," I said, squatting down in front of her. "No

2

ghost here. This really isn't our kind of case. We don't even know his name, and the forensics on this one are going to be important. What can a couple of ghosts do?"

Her smooth brow furrowed and she looked down, a pout on her young face. Emily was still very much a four-year-old at times.

I took her hand and was about to fly us away when the door to the roof opened with a clang. "Sweet-pea," a woman called in a singsong voice. We peered over and saw that she was in her mid-twenties with auburn hair and brown eyes dressed in a tan skirt, heels, and a white blouse. "I've been thinking about this all day, baby." She was quite attractive, I must say, with a beautiful face, generous curves, and a lilting southern accent.

The main part of the building has a high wall—no suicides from up here—but the center of the building went up another ten feet, probably for the elevator machinery, and had a higher roof that has a nice view of Tucson. It's here where we found the body. Not far from it were two lounge chairs, a big beach umbrella, and a cooler.

"I hate these stairs, my God, really I do," the woman said as she slowly climbed the metal stairs to this roof. "With all these holes, I mean, they were not designed for heels."

She had a smile on her red lips when she got to the upper roof and she hoisted a brown bag in her left hand. "For lunch, we've got fettuccine Alfredo, and for dessert…" she trailed off into a chuckle and I glanced at Emily and saw her blushing.

"Sweet-pea, why are you on the ground?" From her angle, the blood wasn't visible yet. She took two more steps, dropped the bag and screamed.

Emily leaned in and looked at the body and then at the woman. "He's got a wedding ring, she doesn't." She

3

paused, a wicked smile on her face, now more the eighty-year-old ghost than the four-year-old kid. Except for her lisp. That is always there. It came out more like "thee doethn't" instead of "she doesn't."

She was watching my face like a hawk and knew she had me. "So, Walter... Fascinating?" she asked.

I had to smile. Not because of the gruesome death or the lascivious details, but because of Emily. Every ghost needed a purpose in their afterlife, and I was lucky that Emily's purpose was me. I nodded. "I guess we've got a case."

She clapped her hands and squealed with joy like only a four-year-old can.

Chapter Two

"FOLLOW HER," I SAID TO EMILY AS SHE LOOKED AT THE retreating woman with the auburn hair. "And call out the Irregulars when you get a chance. We're going to need help."

She nodded, but didn't move right away, her green eyes locking with mine. She stood there, her hands on her hips as she chewed on her lip. She wore her usual shorts and lollipop T-shirt, which were a bit of a mystery in their own right. A ghost, with a little practice, can wear anything they want. Why does Emily always have on those blue shorts and white T-shirt with a colorful lollipop on it? Did she die in that outfit? Was it her favorite? Me, I wear a trench coat and fedora, something Emily had encouraged—with four-year-old vigor—after our first case.

But her outfit was plain, but also advanced. The color of the lollipop was something of an indicator of her mood. It was a pale yellow, reflecting her worry about me.

She didn't talk, she just stared, and I finally noticed the pale-yellow lollipop and figured out what she was waiting for. "I'm fine, Emily," I said, nodding in the direction the woman had fled, the metal door to the roof clanging shut, her sobbing finally out of earshot.

Emily kept chewing on her lip.

"Seriously. A dead body is just my speed right now. And like you said, this is a fascinating case." I ended in the best smile I could, but knew it was a bit strained. "And the sobbing," I added. "I'm just not up for the sobbing."

She nodded, her eyes suddenly sad. Emily knew everything about me and how hard touching back in on Sun's life had been. It had dragged me back through the accident and the fallout from it that had led to our divorce. "I'm worried about you, Walter," she said with a sniff.

"And I'm worried about this case." I squatted down in front of her, modulated my ghostly form just right so I could touch her, and took her hand. "I'll make you a deal. Follow our grieving mistress until she gets to where she's going. Go get the Irregulars and then come back. We'll stick together for this one."

She smiled and nodded and with a "pop" was gone.

After she left, I flew to the edge of the roof and watched the cars crawl below me for a time, wondering at the living. They are going about their days down there, so caught up in the little things, pretending they might not be like me one day.

That didn't last long, though. I quickly got tired of my own moody ghost crap and went to examine the crime scene.

Chapter Three

"THANKS FOR COMING," I SAID TO THE GHOSTS ARRAYED in front of me on the roof of the Tucson high-rise. They go by "Anchor's Irregulars," a homage to Sherlock Holmes and his Baker Street Irregulars. The Anchor part being my last name.

They were a motley collection of ghosts. Fredrick, a natty gentleman who died in 1929 and was the first mortician at our graveyard. Blinky, an overweight geek dressed in a Led Zeppelin T-shirt with glasses, a beer belly, an obsessive love for the game Pac Man, and an insatiable desire for forensics. Anna-Maria, a hot-headed young Hispanic woman on her first case with us. She was dressed in a leather jacket and had recently died after a fall rock climbing up in Flagstaff. And Emily, of course.

Boredom is a serious issue for the dead, so we rarely have trouble finding help when we need it.

"We've got a body," I said, pointing down to the corpse, "a mistress, and a mystery. Blinky, I assume you're good sticking with the body."

He grinned and shook his head enthusiastically. "Absolutely, as long as we get another game of Pac Man in soon." I nodded although I hated it. He would turn the graveyard into a big game of Pac Man and a number of us ghosts would transform our ghostly selves into characters from the game. He was, of course, the red ghost Blinky. My role was Pac Man, and I felt like a fool being chased around the graveyard looking like a huge cheese wheel with a slice cut out of it for a mouth. But I needed him, so I did it.

"Fredrick and Anna-Maria, can you two stay with the mistress? Emily can take you. And one of you break off if another player enters the picture?"

They smiled and nodded.

"Emily and I will stay with the body for now and float around as needed. Let's meet back here at midnight."

Everyone went about their tasks and I was left on the roof with Blinky. I really didn't know much about him beyond his love of video games and geek culture.

"So whatta we got, Boss?" he said, walking over and looking at the body.

"Male, Caucasian, about forty years of age. Married and I am assuming he is an executive since he has access to the roof and set up this little oasis." I nodded to the lounge chairs, umbrella, and cooler. "He's got a cat, he dyes his hair black, presumably to hide the grey, and he appears to have been dropped on the roof from a high enough distance to do this to him."

Blinky nodded and got his face up close and examined minute details of the body, just as I had done. "Some minor scrapes on his fingers," he said, pointing at his right hand.

I nodded. "Maybe sign of a struggle." I let Blinky examine the body while I slowly went over the roof. Ghosts are good at this kind of thing. We see without eyes—something for you philosophy buffs to ponder—but we all see really well. Blinky's round, wire-frame glasses were part of his ghostly form, not real. We could look at things very closely and we weren't subject to the heat of the day or assaulted by the smells I'm sure were starting to emanate from the body.

I didn't find anything interesting on the roof and Blinky didn't see anything else on the body. "So how the hell did he get here?" he asked, looking up.

I shrugged. "Helicopter? Hot air balloon? Drones?"

He shook his head. "Too heavy for drones."

"That part doesn't really matter," I said.

"What? Why?"

"The murder was elaborate, difficult to pull off. The murderer wanted this death to be all over the papers, wanted to embarrass our stiff here."

Blinky rubbed at his stubbly face. "The wife?"

I shrugged my shoulders. "Until we know who these people are, there's not much more to do."

I heard sirens below, the police were here. I went about examining the scene one more time before they started tromping all over it.

Chapter Four

WHEN EMILY CAME BACK FROM TAKING FREDRICK AND Anna-Maria to the mistress, we left Blinky with the corpse and started roaming the office building. A strange murder on their roof was bound to be talked about.

As ghosts, we can't interview the living—the dead, that's another story—but we can listen and observe. And if we are tailing someone, forget about it. We will never leave you no matter where you go. You can't lose us, it's just not possible. If you're hiding something, we will find it.

One of these days, I keep thinking the Tucson PD will wise up and start partnering with us in a formal way. Emily and I, we've solved a bunch of murders now. When it's all over, I go to the SECI chamber—that typewriter for ghosts Tamara Watson and Jin Shi invented while PhD students at the University of Arizona—bang out these stories and Tamara gets them to a detective that's open to getting leads from ghosts. It's been a few years now that ghosts have been using the SECI chamber for everything from telling their wife where the latest will is, to little stories like mine, to full blown memoirs. The SECI chamber has changed the world. The dead know it; the living haven't quite figured it out yet.

As we walked the cubes, conference rooms, and swank offices on the top floor, we kept hearing the name Andrew and it didn't take long to figure out he was the boss up here. Andrew Verner of Verner and Associates. A law firm.

"Awwww," Emily said pointing at his portrait in the glitzy waiting area. "He's quite handsome without his face mushed in."

And I guess he was. Ice-blue eyes, short black hair, a cleft chin.

"The mistress is Elizabeth Sills," Fredrick said, walking up to us with Anna-Maria by his side. And yes, we can all fly, but we walk when we can. Acting more like the living helps keep us out of that gape-jawed ghostly hell called the bardo. "She's from Georgia, been in Tucson for four years and worked as Verner's executive assistant. Not much there yet," he added. "She's absolutely inconsolable."

I thanked Fredrick for the update and he went back to Elizabeth just as the police came streaming in. Two detectives and a bunch of uniforms. I guess they were taking this murder seriously.

"Oh my. *Bello*," Anna-Maria said, eyeing Detective Alvarez—Tamara Watson's contact in the Tucson PD— with obvious hunger. "Can I have him, Walter? Please!" Her brown eyes lit up and she had a big smile on her face.

"Knock yourself out, kid," I said, and Anna-Maria glued herself to the handsome detective.

Emily rolled her eyes. "She's still so young."

I nodded. Emily meant young as a ghost, still entranced by the physical which tends to fade with time. I looked back at the portrait of Andrew Verner and his tight smile and sighed. "He's a lawyer, and you know what that means…"

"Anyone could have done it!" Emily finished with her eyes bright.

Chapter Five

"It's not her," I said the moment I laid eyes on Victoria Hall-Verner. She was older than her husband, over fifty, with an elegant, cultured air to her. She wore a dark skirt, a mauve blouse, and a strand of pearls around her neck. She came from money, that was clear.

We were in her expansive living room with white leather couches, a gas fireplace, and big windows looking out onto the cactus-covered Catalina Mountains. There was a baby grand piano there with family portraits on it. Nothing remarkable except it appeared the Verners didn't have any children.

Detective Alvarez had just given her the news flanked by Detective Jones. He is medium height and muscular with short cropped hair and a black mustache. She's petite with dark skin and her curly black hair barely contained in a ponytail.

Victoria's hands shook as they sat clasped in her lap and she sucked in a deep breath and held it for too long, but she stayed steady, asked questions, remained focused.

"He's so kind," Anna-Maria said, referring to Alvarez's quiet, calm delivery. Emily rolled her eyes.

The interview was short and I was sure she was innocent, but we waited until *the* question got asked.

Alvarez cleared his throat and swallowed hard. "Mrs. Verner, do you know Elizabeth Sills?"

She gave him a dismissing look. "His *personal* assistant. Yes, of course." Alvarez took a breath to ask another question, but she held up her hand. "I know about the affair, and while it didn't have my blessing, I did nothing to stop it. Andy needed to… wander from time to time. It never lasted long, he always came back to me." The look on her face was pure confidence, the kind of look no one has ever seen on my face unless it was for an acting role.

"You called it, Walter," Emily said.

"Do you know anyone that would have wanted to hurt your husband?" Jones asked as she adjusted her glasses. "Anyone that would have wanted to do so in such a"—she pursed her full lips, searching for an adjective delicate and yet forceful enough to describe what had happened—"in such an *unusual* way?"

Mrs. Hall-Verner took a deep breath and bit her lower lip, the first break in her tight demeanor. "I suspect it was me they wanted to hurt, not him. They must want the affair in the tabloids, which will be a terrible embarrassment to me. Most of the money is mine, you see." She ended in a sniff.

Emily elbowed me, her smile big and her eyes sparkling. This had gone from bizarre to lascivious, straight to money and power. It really didn't get much better than this.

Chapter Six

WE GATHERED AT MIDNIGHT ON THE ROOF OF THE Tucson high-rise, the site of the murder. Ghosts love their graveyards, and our time is midnight. We are more awake, a bit more powerful. We feel it coming, we naturally tend to gather. Our graveyard has the "Midnight Circle" which is kind of like an old-fashioned campfire gathering where we share stories, put on plays—mostly Shakespeare—and socialize. The living are asleep, the dead are awake. It's a good time of day for us.

We met at the crime scene partially to avoid the distractions of the Midnight Circle and partially because it just seemed like the right place. The area was cordoned off with yellow "Crime Scene" tape and a few numbered yellow markers on the roof and the outline of where Andrew Verner's body had been found.

"Emily, if you don't mind," I said. She loved this "sum it all up" detective thing. She paced in front of the Irregulars, her hands clasped behind her back, a serious look on her young face.

"We're deep into the rich upper crust of Tucson

society here, my friends, maybe even treading into the US military. Our working theory is that the murder was aimed at destabilizing Victoria Hall-Verner, a major shareholder in Raytheon Missile Systems and the owner of the local ABC television station. We know it took money to pull this off." She pointed to the outline of Verner's body and then poked her thumb upwards. "The cops are going to have a hell of a time with this one, so it's up to us. We've got to go where they can't and figure this thing out."

I smiled as I watched her. Maybe as a younger ghost she hung out in theatres for most of the forties, watching *The Maltese Falcon*, *The Big Sleep*, the Thin Man movies, and the like. Whatever it was, she just loved this stuff, and it was a good distraction for me.

And she thankfully wasn't shy about her lisp. Not a bit. Taking on phrases like "Raytheon Missile Systems" even though it came out as "Raytheon Mithile Thythem." The "System" was pretty mangled and even as well as I know her made it even harder to not think of her as an adorable little girl.

"Blinky, what do we know about the death?" she asked.

Blinky nodded. "This is a little twisted, guys. Someone wanted Verner to suffer. He was dropped from a height of fifty to a hundred feet, but likely no more than that. He didn't die right away. They found traces of a sedative in his bloodstream and the coroner believes it wore off before he died a slow, painful death. The time of death is approximately 10:30 a.m., but the coroner believes that the fall occurred some hours before that between 5 a.m. and 9 a.m."

Emily looked thoughtful. "So that means the drop could have occurred under the cover of darkness, making the mechanics of this much simpler." She turned to Anna-

Maria. "When was the last time Mrs. Verner saw her husband?"

Anna-Maria didn't hesitate, rolling out the details as if she had an eidetic memory—one of the benefits of being a ghost. Without our bodies, our memories are very sharp. "He left the house at 5:30 a.m., the time he normally heads to the gym, but he never arrived. No one saw him in the office that morning either. After the gym, he was scheduled for a breakfast meeting and then an early round of golf with a client. He did not attend any of those." Emily nodded, turning towards Fredrick, but Anna-Maria added, "Can I get back to Sebastián… I mean, Detective Alvarez? You know… just in case something happens in the night?"

Emily looked at me and I nodded and Anna-Maria flew off into the night. "That girl…" she said, shaking her head.

"She'll learn," I said. I was fond of Anna-Maria's newly dead enthusiasm. She hadn't found out why she was a ghost and if there was any unfinished business for her to attend to. It made her rather refreshing compared to the likes of me.

"And Ms. Sills, the mistress?" Emily asked, turning to Fredrick.

"She is grieving, deeply, poor dear, and is certainly not the murderer, but…"

He took a step closer. Fredrick was fairly central in the graveyard not only because he had started it back in the thirties, but because he was a well-seasoned, dependable ghost and was very perceptive when it came to human behavior.

And this is another area where ghosts have an edge over the living. Without all the dense flesh, we have a well-developed intuition, and in some instances, something a bit more. I don't want to say we're psychic, let's just say that as spirits without bodies we are more sensitive to what is going on around us. Banquo, a ghost back at the graveyard that helps new ghosts acclimate, calls this "awareness."

Fredrick took a deep breath, not that ghosts breathe, but flesh equivalents still hold power for us. He was gathering his thoughts. "I believe we can leave young Elizabeth Sills to her grief, but I think we need to take a closer look at her former lover, a man named William Costa. Elizabeth called him earlier and..." he shook his head. "He's married too. She called him 'Sweet-Pea.' Poor girl seems to have a thing for married men. They hadn't talked in a while and she still feels something for him. Well, I don't see a clear motive, but there was something about his tone. He didn't seem that surprised."

Chapter Seven

"HE DID IT," EMILY SAID, POINTING AT WILLIAM COSTA as he teed off at the Tucson Country Club, a bright green golf course backed by the cactus-covered Santa Catalina Mountains. "He hated Verner for stealing his mistress, was desperate to get her back." This was something of a game Emily and I played as we tried to hone our instincts, our awareness as ghost detectives. "That's why the elaborate setup and bizarre conditions of the murder."

He was tall and thin, handsome with dark hair and too-white teeth, and at least ten years older than Elizabeth Sills. He wore brand-name apparel and swung expensive clubs, and he was a skilled golfer.

It was just Emily and me. Fredrick was helping to acclimate a new ghost back at the graveyard—always a difficult transition. Anna-Maria was still haunting Detective Alvarez—and let's be honest, that's what it was at this point, but at least it was a kind haunting, but something we would have to keep an eye on. Blinky was still with the medical examiner as the formal autopsy was continuing today.

I nodded. I felt it too. This was our guy, but I wasn't buying the jealousy motivation. There was something else going on here.

And so began our 24/7 tail of William Costa. No matter what he did and where he went, we were with him. Listening to his phone conversations, reading his texts, watching what he ate, watching him while he slept, we were even with him in the bathroom or when he made love to his wife or one of his mistresses. Those last two duties were strictly my territory. Unpleasant, yes, but I would not ask a woman to watch a man go to the toilet, and with Emily having died at four, watching human biological reproductive urges in action was out of the question. I've been dead long enough, and am sufficiently distanced from my biology, that I don't find the latter either titillating or even interesting.

William Costa owned a series of car dealerships, and while he was wealthy, it was not nearly on the scale of the Verners. Although, he did have enough to rent a helicopter with ease.

The first day was golf, lunch with his mistress, including a recreational trip to the bathroom during which Emily excused herself and checked in with the other Irregulars, a few hours at the office, and then dinner with his wife.

The next day he worked most of the day and had dinner with a different mistress. The day after that he flew to Las Vegas for a business meeting, lost about $10,000 playing craps, and flew home.

I was so sick of this guy. He was shallow, narcissistic, and totally annoying. I was beginning to wonder if we had the right guy, and really wondering about Elizabeth's taste in men. Anna-Maria had kept us in the loop on the official investigation, and they were looking into business rivals and associates of Victoria Hall-Verner, but it was progressing slowly. The tabloids, in the meantime, had caught wind of the story and it had gone national with the kind of headlines you would expect. "Mystery Death on top of Tucson Skyscraper," "It's Raining Men," a gem from one of the tabloids, and "Gruesome Death in one of Tucson's Richest Families."

"I don't know, kid," I said to Emily as we followed William down the hallway of a Toyota dealership. He had been meeting with his manager and had excused himself to go to the bathroom.

But he didn't stop at the bathroom. He strolled back to the garage and did what he called one of his pop inspections. We had seen this a few times before; it's his way of keeping all his employees on their toes.

But this one didn't look right. He went up to a mechanic, a young man with a brown ponytail and tuft of beard under his lip, walked under the lift holding up a Tundra pickup, and started asking questions about the oil change he was doing. His words were stilted and forced. Before he had only done a quick walkthrough, not actually having a conversation with any other employees.

"You were saying…" Emily said with a grin. The lollipop on her shirt was back to its usual cherry red. It had turned red and stayed this way since the case got good. The girl does love murder.

We watched closely and we caught the exchange. When Costa went to leave, he pressed a small key into the young man's hand and headed out of the garage.

"Looks like we gotta split up, Emily. Who do you want?"

She nodded to the young man. "I can't stand Costa, sorry, Walter, but he's all yours."

I shook my head and followed William Costa to the

toilet and watched him text his two mistresses while he took a dump, once again glad ghosts can't smell.

Chapter Eight

A FEW HOURS LATER, EMILY POPPED IN—SOMETHING I still couldn't do reliably. "Anything going on here?" she asked. We were in a swank restaurant with William and mistress number two.

I shook my head.

"Good," she said, grabbing my hand, and with a "pop" we were at the airport. It used to be disorienting, the whole jump from one spot to another, but I'm used to it now. Emily is very good at it, it doesn't seem to be difficult at all for her. I did it recently, but it was almost by accident and revolved around my desperate need to see my ex-wife Sun.

"There," she said, pointing at a helicopter. "Scene of the crime."

There was a middle-aged, blond-haired man who was in the pilot's seat with his headset on and looked like he was doing a preflight check. The helicopter had a big nine on it and the ABC logo.

"This is Victoria Hall-Verner's station," I said.

"Yup. I followed the money, boss. Our boy from the garage took that key to the greyhound bus station and

23

opened a locker. There was an envelope and a small bag in there. He pocketed the envelope and carried the bag to El Presidio Park, stuffed it in a trash can, and fifteen minutes later this bozo came and picked it up. Bing, bam, boom. We got 'em!"

She raised her hand for a high five and I slapped her hand and nodded, but we didn't have all the pieces yet. We had the players, and knew in broad strokes what had happened, but it wasn't enough; we didn't know why. "Any physical evidence in the chopper?" I asked. The rotors were starting to spin, the helicopter probably headed up for a rush hour traffic report.

Emily shook her head, her Shirley Temple curls bouncing in the most adorable way. "Can't you go write it up, get Tamara to reach out to Alvarez?"

I bit my lip and thought about it. There wasn't any real motive. William Costa hadn't had contact with Elizabeth Sills for months. Did he even know about her affair with Andrew Verner? And this helicopter put the focus on Victoria Hall-Verner who did know about her husband's affair, and jealousy there was a real possibility, although she certainly didn't present that way. The cops might be able to get a confession out of the helicopter pilot, but they might not. My guess is that the helicopter was clean and there wouldn't be any physical evidence.

"Not quite," I told her, sad to see the smile melt from her face. "Stick with him a while longer and meet us at the murder site at midnight. I've got an idea."

Chapter Nine

ON THE ROOF, THE NIGHTTIME LIGHTS OF TUCSON arrayed before us, I let Emily bring the Irregulars up to speed while I stared at the lights. They were so orderly, so calm, they hid the seething stew of human frailty and weakness below. We were this team of ghosts, not a one with any formal training, whiling away their afterlives solving murders. I had been a dentist and before that an actor. Fredrick, who I was glad to see back, was a mortician. Anna-Maria had been a student up north at NAU. And Blinky, I didn't even know what he did. But yet here we were working as a team orchestrated by the ancient Emily who looked like a four-year-old, innocent-as-can-be little girl.

"So we know William Costa is behind the murder and the easy bet is he did it because Verner's mistress, Elizabeth Sills, is his former mistress," I said. "But I don't buy it. The elaborate murder is a misdirect towards Victoria Hall-Verner, even down to the helicopter used. We are missing a piece of this and I want to try something a little different, so new assignments." Anna-Maria looked sad, but the others nodded.

"Don't worry, Anna-Maria, you get to stick with Alvarez, but I need you to come up with three facts about him that aren't common knowledge, and this is important, aren't embarrassing. Emily will be around in an hour to get them from you."

She nodded and flew off.

"Fredrick, can you go find Elizabeth Sills and stick with her? I've got a hunch there is something else going on there, maybe something at the office. She's..." I shrugged my shoulders not having the words, but something wasn't right there. He nodded and popped away.

"And Blinky, I need you in the law office. Go there tonight, read every piece of paper you can see, listen to every conversation in the morning." He opened his mouth up to speak, but I held my hand up. This wasn't his area, he only wanted to hang with cops or coroners. "I know this means more Pac Man time for me. Trust me, it's important."

He nodded and sunk down into the building—the Verner and Associates offices were below us.

That left Emily and me alone on the roof and I stared back out at the lights. This wasn't a bad afterlife, we were doing some good, but I was starting to understand why all the movie detectives seemed to be rather world weary.

"Hey, Boss?" Emily asked.

"What?"

"Why'd you tell Anna-Maria to not give us any embarrassing information on Alvarez?"

I shook my head and smiled. "Because I don't want to know if he has a mole on his right butt cheek."

Emily's jaw dropped and I laughed. "You don't think... she wouldn't..."

26

"Honey, she was twenty when she died, and that was only a few weeks ago. Of course she's seen him in the shower."

She shook her head. "She's a pistol, that one." She watched the lights with me for a while and then asked, "What about us?"

"It's time to wake Tamara Watson up."

Chapter Ten

THERE ARE THREE SECI CHAMBERS IN THE AFTERLIFE Communications building that Tamara and her partner Jin started after they got their PhDs. They are crowded now, a line of ghosts a week long all waiting to try their hand at the ghost keyboard to get their messages out. That works for a normal case; it wouldn't work here. We needed real-time communication to pull this off.

Tamara had told me of the next generation SECI chamber they were building and told me to use it in an emergency. This was an emergency. The SECI chamber is a bit larger than a phone booth and is made out of this high-tech material that shields all electromagnetic radia-tion. We ghosts, you guessed it, emanate electromagnetic energy at an extremely high frequency. The old SECI chamber required ghosts to do some bizarre contortions of their forms—not nearly as bizarre as becoming Pac Man— and not all ghosts can do it. The 2.0 SECI chamber has a huge keyboard that you place your fingers through the keys and it detects the EM radiation and your words appear on the monitor above. This one is, literally, a keyboard for ghosts.

When we got there, I wrote a short message, "911." This would wake up Tamara, who could monitor all the SECI chambers from her house, and we could, essentially, text each other.

"We need Detective Alvarez now," I said to Emily. "We need the helicopter pilot and the mechanic arrested and interrogated. We need the forensics team going over the helicopter. We need him to start looking at William Costa's financial records for the pilot payoff."

Emily looked puzzled. In the past, we had solved the case and then told the police.

"Look, Costa was smart," I continued. "He was very careful. The pilot probably doesn't know who hired him to dump Verner's body on that building. We need the smoking gun, kid."

Emily nodded. "Now go get me those three facts from Anna-Maria. I need Alvarez to really believe in ghosts." She walked out of the chamber; popping was not possible inside.

Text appeared on the monitor. "Walter is that you? What's going on."

"Sorry to wake you, Tamara," I typed back. "We need you to help us catch a murderer."

"What can I do?"

"Wake Detective Alvarez up. First we are going to prove that ghosts are real and then we are going to work directly with him to catch a murderer."

There was a pause of fifteen minutes and I was getting worried. Was this too much for her? I knew that not everyone was happy about ghosts communicating from beyond the pale and that Tamara was getting hate mail and worse.

"Sorry for the delay," she typed back. "I had to fiddle with my gear. I've routed your messages to my phone and can reply too. Heading over to Alvarez's house right now. Let's do this!"

Chapter Eleven

"Do you know this man?" Detective Alvarez asked Elizabeth Sills in the cramped interrogation room. The picture was a mugshot of a young man with a brown ponytail and a tuft of facial hair under his lip, the mechanic that William Costa had passed the key to.

She dabbed at her eyes, swollen and red from crying, and shook her head. Even in this state she was beautiful. It kind of helped make all of this make sense. She used her beauty to get what she wanted.

We had worked all night and most of the day. I typed to Tamara, she relayed to Detectives Alvarez and Jones, and she texted me back. Emily popped to all the Irregulars, giving them assignments and coordinating the activities and then updating me, and I would pass on the information.

We had been a part of the arrest of Vince Smith, the helicopter pilot, and Ian Stoltz, the garage mechanic. Both were sitting in nearby interrogation rooms. We had searched their residences—a ghost doesn't need a search warrant—helped the police find them. We applied our intuitive senses, our ghostly awareness, to help guide the questioning. It had been magnificent.

All of us were here watching, except for Blinky who was still at the Verner and Associates offices.

"That's odd," Detective Jones said, leaning back in her metal chair. "We pulled GPS data from his phone. He's been at your condo four times in the last month, but only for a few minutes each time." She leaned forward. "Long enough to hand something off. Like a note, maybe?"

Her smooth brow wrinkled and she looked indignant, her southern lilt becoming more clipped. "I do not know what you are implying here. I do not know that man."

Alvarez smiled. "Oh, but he knows you." He slid forward a picture of the two of them mugging for a selfie, and Elizabeth's cheeks flushed red. "You see, I think you and Mr. Costa are smart. No cell phones. No digital trail. Just notes passed and then destroyed like two kids in class." He showed her a plastic bag with the remnants of a burnt note that had a few letters still visible: "Verne," "rooft," and "$100,." Fredrick had witnessed Elizabeth cleaning out her condo and noticed the burned notes. The police hadn't even needed a warrant to get at her trash, but it did provide what they needed for the warrant they used to search her condo.

Her nostrils flared and she crossed her arms over her chest and suddenly she didn't look like she was grieving anymore; she looked furious. I was impressed. This girl was a fine actress, she could have gone far in Hollywood with those looks and that talent. Well… before she conspired to commit murder, that is.

"She fooled me," Fredrick said, shaking his head.

"With a dreamboat like that," Emily said, "how could you help yourself?"

"Verner couldn't," I added. "Or Costa."

"Here's what bugs me," Alvarez said. "Costa is not a nice guy. He's married. He has two, count them two, mistresses. Seems to be that Verner was an upgrade for you. Why did you guys kill him?"

Elizabeth Sills sat there fuming, her red lips clamped tight. I had no idea why they had done it. This was the one piece of the puzzle we were lacking.

"We've got Vince Smith, the helicopter pilot," Alvarez said. "Found Verner's hairs in the helicopter and some threads from the seats on Verner. Smith is talking, he made a deal, maybe you should too."

That last part was a lie. Smith didn't know who hired him, he picked up Verner unconscious in the trunk of a car in a parking garage. Everything was anonymous handoffs. The car had been stolen and was a dead end.

"I think I'll be executing my constitutional right to representation at this time," Elizabeth said.

Chapter Twelve

"IT'S QUITE SIMPLE, REALLY," BLINKY SAID, A PROUD look on his round face. We were in Andrew Verner's swank office while the detectives pulled the contents out of his wall safe.

"Our Ms. Sills was looking to upgrade from mistress to wife, but Verner would not leave his wife, and the more she pressured him, the more distant he became and the more time he'd spend with his wife. Although, he couldn't quite let go of the lovely Elizabeth Sills."

I gave him a questioning look and he gestured around the office. "You should hear the gossip around this place." There was a crowd outside the window-lined wall staring at the proceedings.

I nodded for him to continue.

"The 'marry me thing' was going on about three months ago. A few weeks ago, she started having a bit of an upset stomach every morning," Blinky said, his eyebrows wagging above his glasses.

"Preggers!" Emily shouted and then put her hand to

her mouth and looked around embarrassed as if the people in the office could hear her.

"I've seen her stomach problems, too," Fredrick offered. "I just thought it was from the trauma."

"Verner set up a trust for his child," Blinky continued, "a multimillion-dollar trust with Ms. Sills in control of it. She was set."

I shrugged. "Sounds like she got most of what she wanted. Why pull Costa in, why kill Verner?"

Blinky shrugged. "No clue, just know that this is the next layer of the onion and they needed to know about it." He pointed at the detectives.

"This is interesting," Detective Jones said, opening a manila folder. "Ms. Sills didn't mention this. Verner set up a trust in her name, for… for their child."

Alvarez grabbed the folder, his eyes snapping back and forth as he read it. "I think we need to have another conversation with Ms. Sills and Mrs. Hall-Verner."

Chapter Thirteen

A CAREER MISTRESS UPGRADING TO RICHER AND RICHER men. When she thinks she's gone as high as she can, she tries to become the wife. When that doesn't work she gets pregnant and secures a fat trust fund. And then she... kills the father? Why? Because she's nuts and still loves the last man down the totem pole and he helps her kill the father?

We were missing something.

I was pacing the roof in front of my team on the high-rise at midnight. The interviews with Elizabeth Sills and Victoria Hall-Verner hadn't yielded anything useful. Sills had admitted to the trust and the pregnancy, but she had been correct when she had said, "That ain't no crime."

Mrs. Hall-Verner had been shocked to hear of the pregnancy and the trust, but it didn't change anything. She had provided evidence—text messages, restaurant dates, gifts—that confirmed that Verner was spending more time with her and winding down his affair. She claimed to not care about the child.

"We got Costa, they arrested him today," Emily said.

"We got the pilot, too. This is good, Walter, this is really good."

I shook my head; it wasn't enough. I wanted to see our southern belle, Elizabeth Sills, in jail too. We had the burned notes from Costa, but that wasn't enough.

"Perhaps if we took a night off," Fredrick suggested, ever with the level head.

I ignored them all and kept pacing. Two love triangles with Sills a part of both, four people, and one baby.

One baby!

It hit me in a flash. "I got it!" I said. "Time to wake everyone up again."

Chapter Fourteen

THE INTERROGATION ROOM WAS TOO SMALL FOR THE crowd, so this was happening in the plain precinct conference room. A scarred wooden table, creaky chairs, a whiteboard and a coffee machine. There were the two detectives, William Costa, Elizabeth Sills, and Victoria Hall-Verner, as well as three different lawyers. Emily and I had gone back to the SECI chamber, woken Tamara up, typed up what I had figured out, and Tamara had facilitated a conversation between me and Detective Alvarez. It was time to watch the detectives execute our plan.

"Mr. Costa, you are going to jail," Alvarez said, starting the ball rolling. "We can link you directly to the murder via Ian Stoltz. He made himself a nice deal and we know all the little errands he ran for you." Costa looked great in his grey prison jumpsuit, a sour look on his face.

"Including," Detective Jones began, licking her lips, "his deliveries from Mrs. Hall-Verner to you."

Victoria's face was hard and she was dressed elegantly in a silk blouse and cashmere sweater even at this early 6:00 a.m. hour.

"You see, you all had the same problem," Alvarez said, sliding out the portrait of Andrew Verner. "Mr. Costa, you wanted her back," he said pointing at Sills.

Jones looked at Sills. "And your baby-daddy was about to dissolve the trust, so you had a problem." She slid a manila envelope halfway across the table. Elizabeth Sill's eyes got wide. This was a wild guess we had, but Verner's lawyer had confirmed it.

"And you," Alvarez said, looking at Mrs. Hall-Verner, "got rid of your embarrassing little problem—a bastard heir to the Hall fortune."

I smiled. That was the piece that had come to me up on the roof. Andrew and Victoria didn't have any children, and while she could tolerate an affair, she couldn't tolerate an heir by another woman.

Victoria's face stayed stony as she stared at Alvarez.

"The pilot, Vince Smith," Alvarez said, "is cooperating. He's got a nice deal, too." He looked at Victoria, and here is where he had to bluff. Smith didn't know anything, but the other two didn't know that. "You see, you made a mistake. You used Smith before, he knows all about—"

"There is no financial trail leading to me," Costa said, rising from his seat, his handcuffed wrists in front of him. His lawyer gave him the don't-say-anything-else look, but he continued, his hand stabbing out at Victoria. "It was her money, her plan. I have proof!"

"He's right," Elizabeth said, her face red. "She promised me ten million if I helped, if we put William on the birth certificate. Played nice with Andrew for a while longer. Arranged our rooftop reunion. You didn't think anyone could unravel a murder this bizarre."

And then they were all shouting at each other, the three conspirators laying it all out in front of two detectives despite their lawyers' attempts to keep them quiet.

I smiled. We got them, we got them all.

Chapter Fifteen

It was a very special Midnight Circle and I watched proudly as the Irregulars took center stage among the gravestones under a gibbous moon surrounded by ghosts and told the lascivious, decidedly human details of our case.

Emily wasn't here, but I don't worry about her. She knows her way around the afterlife.

They asked me to join them, but I demurred. I used to be an actor, was even in an episode of *Buffy the Vampire Slayer*, but I wanted this to be their moment.

Fredrick narrated and Blinky and Anna-Maria played the parts of the characters in this little tragic play. Anna-Maria even going so far as flying up into the night sky and slamming her ghostly body into the ground to illustrate how the victim died.

The ghosts went wild. A gruesome murder and tragic human failings are like candy to us who have lost our lives and are earthbound spirits. It's one of the reasons Shakespeare goes over so well.

Banquo was there. He's a bald, big-bellied guy who is

more or less the leader around here. He created the Midnight Circle, directs all the plays, and he's helped out most of the ghosts that have died since he came here. I, though, am not a big fan. He and his chosen few are kind of like the varsity team, and my Irregulars and I are definitely not the cool kids. That, and Emily. She has a massive crush on him and I know if he ever asked her to help him, she would leave me in a second.

Banquo caught my eye at the end of the performance as the ghosts hooted, hollered, and whistled—we aren't much for clapping given our incorporeal nature. He smiled and nodded as if to say good job. I probably would have gone over to receive his praise, but then the Irregulars were there and I was congratulating them and celebrating our victory.

It was a new step for us working directly with Detectives Alvarez and Jones, the living and the dead doing what neither could have done alone.

After the circle dissipated, I asked Anna-Maria to walk with me. "You did good on your first outing with us," I said.

Her brown eyes were bright. "Thanks for giving me a chance, Boss."

I nodded. "And I'd like to bring you on permanently as one of Anchor's Irregulars, but…"

Her face fell and her eyes widened.

"You've got to stop haunting Detective Alvarez."

"I… He… You know, I just…"

I laughed and stopped walking. "Look, I get it. He's a handsome guy, you're a young woman, but it's not good for you. The flesh is gone. It's not coming back. The sooner you understand that the better this will be."

She bit her lip and nodded.

I was opening my mouth to speak again when there

42

was a sharp "pop" and Emily was there, panting as if she had just run a long ways, her cheeks red.

"Walter. You're… You're not going to believe what I found. Holy mackerel, this one, it's… it's…"

"A fascinating murder?" I offered.

Her eyes widened and her lisp was thick. "It's a double murder and… well… you just have to see it. Right now, before the cops get there." She reached her hand out to me, so eager for the next case, and how could I resist?

I looked at Anna-Maria. "Do we have a deal?"

She hesitated, for just a moment, and then smiled and nodded. "Yes, no more haunting Detective Alvarez."

"Let's go," I said, taking both of their hands, and with a "pop" we were off to our next case.

More Mystery?

WALTER AND EMILY HAVE A LOT MORE CASES TO SOLVE. Next is "**Death of a Dentist**," available May, 2020. Join my email newsletter and never miss a thing.

Death of a Dentist

Walter Anchor spends his afterlife solving murders in the hope of one day solving the toughest murder of all. His own.

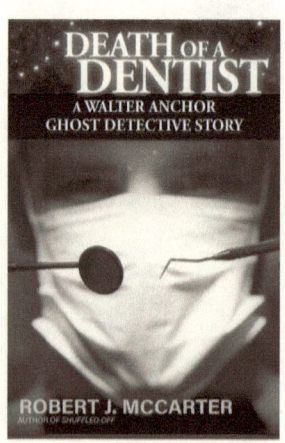

But when his partner and best ghost-friend Emily convinces him to relive his last few days to find a lead in his very cold case, everything changes. He finds a past and his relationships much more complicated than he remembered and uncovers an unthinkable clue. A clue, that if followed, would force him to reevaluate his life and his afterlife.

.From the author of *Shuffled Off: A Ghost's Memoir* comes a mystery unlike anything seen before.

Get "Death of a Dentist" Now!

About the Author

Robert J. McCarter is the author of seven novels, three novellas, and dozens of short stories. He is a finalist for the *Writers of the Future* contest and his stories have appeared or are forthcoming in *The Saturday Evening Post, Pulphouse Fiction Magazine, Fiction River, Andromeda Spaceways Inflight Magazine,* and numerous anthologies.

His latest effort is a serialized novel called *Woody and June Versus the Apocalypse*, a story of adventure and love and taking things (even the apocalypse) in stride. Of his novel, *Seeing Forever*, Kirkus Reviews says, "Sci-fi as it should be: engaging, moving, and grand in scope."

He lives in the mountains of Arizona with his amazing wife and his ridiculously adorable dogs.

Find out more at:
robertjmccarter.com

Books by Robert J. McCarter

Walter Anchor, Ghost Detective Stories

- **Case 1: Detecting Haley** (also part of *Life After: Stories of Life, Death, and the Places in Between*)
- **Case 2: The Ghost Bride's Gift**
- **Case 3: A Long Hard Fall**
- **Case 4: Death of a Dentist** (coming May, 2020)
- **Case 5: A Hollywood Kind of a Murder** (coming July 2020)
- **Case 6: The Red Arrow Murders** (coming September, 2020)
- **Unfinished Business: The Cases of Walter Anchor Ghost Detective** (coming October, 2020)

For a complete list of Walter Anchor stories, go to RobertJMcCarter.com/WalterAnchor

Novels in the "Ghost's Memoir" world:

- Shuffled Off: A Ghost's Memoir, Book 1
- Drawing the Dead
- To Be a Fool: A Ghost's Memoir, Book 2
- Of Things Not Seen: A Ghost's Memoir, Book 3
- A Boy, a Girl, and a Ghost

For a complete list the "Ghost's Memoir" novels, go to ShuffledOff.com

The Wood and June versus the Apocalypse series

Find out more at WoodyAndJune.com

The Neutrinoman and Lightningirl Series

Find out more at Neutrinoman.com

Other Novels:

- Seeing Forever

For a more information, go to RobertJMcCarter.com